W9-AVW-149

To Enid Willow

American edition published in 2017 by Andersen Press USA,
an imprint of Andersen Press Ltd.
www.andersenpressusa.com

First published in Great Britain in 2017 by Andersen Press Ltd.,
20 Vauxhall Bridge Road, London SW1V 2SA.

Copyright © David McKee, 2017

All rights reserved. No part of this book may be reproduced, stored in a retrieval system, or transmitted in any form or by any means—electronic, mechanical, photocopying, recording, or otherwise—without the prior written permission of Andersen Press Ltd., except for the inclusion of brief quotations in an acknowledged review.

Distributed in the United States and Canada by
Lerner Publishing Group, Inc.
241 First Avenue North
Minneapolis, MN 55401 USA

For reading levels and more information, look up this title at www.lernerbooks.com.

Color separated in Switzerland by Photolitho AG, Zürich.
Printed and bound in Malaysia.

Library of Congress Cataloging-in-Publication Data Available
ISBN: 978-1-5124-8124-2
eBook ISBN: 978-1-5124-8139-6

1–TWP–7/15/2017

ELMER

and the Tune

David McKee

Andersen Press USA

East Bridgewater Public Library
32 Union Street
East Bridgewater, MA 02333
(508) 378-1616
www.eastbridgewaterlibrary.org

Elmer, the patchwork elephant, was taking a walk when his young friend Rose appeared, humming a tune.

"That's a catchy tune, Rose," said Elmer.

"Yes," said Rose. "It's so catchy I can't get it out of my head." By the time they went their different ways, Elmer was also humming the tune.

"Good morning, Elmer," said Lion. "I like that tune you're humming."

"I got it from Rose," said Elmer. "Now I can't stop humming it."

Elmer went on his way, and Lion started humming the tune.

A little later, Elmer met Hippo. Hippo was also humming the tune.

“Hello, Hippo,” said Elmer. “I hear that Rose came by.”

“How did you know?” asked Hippo.

“The tune,” said Elmer, going on his way. “The tune.”

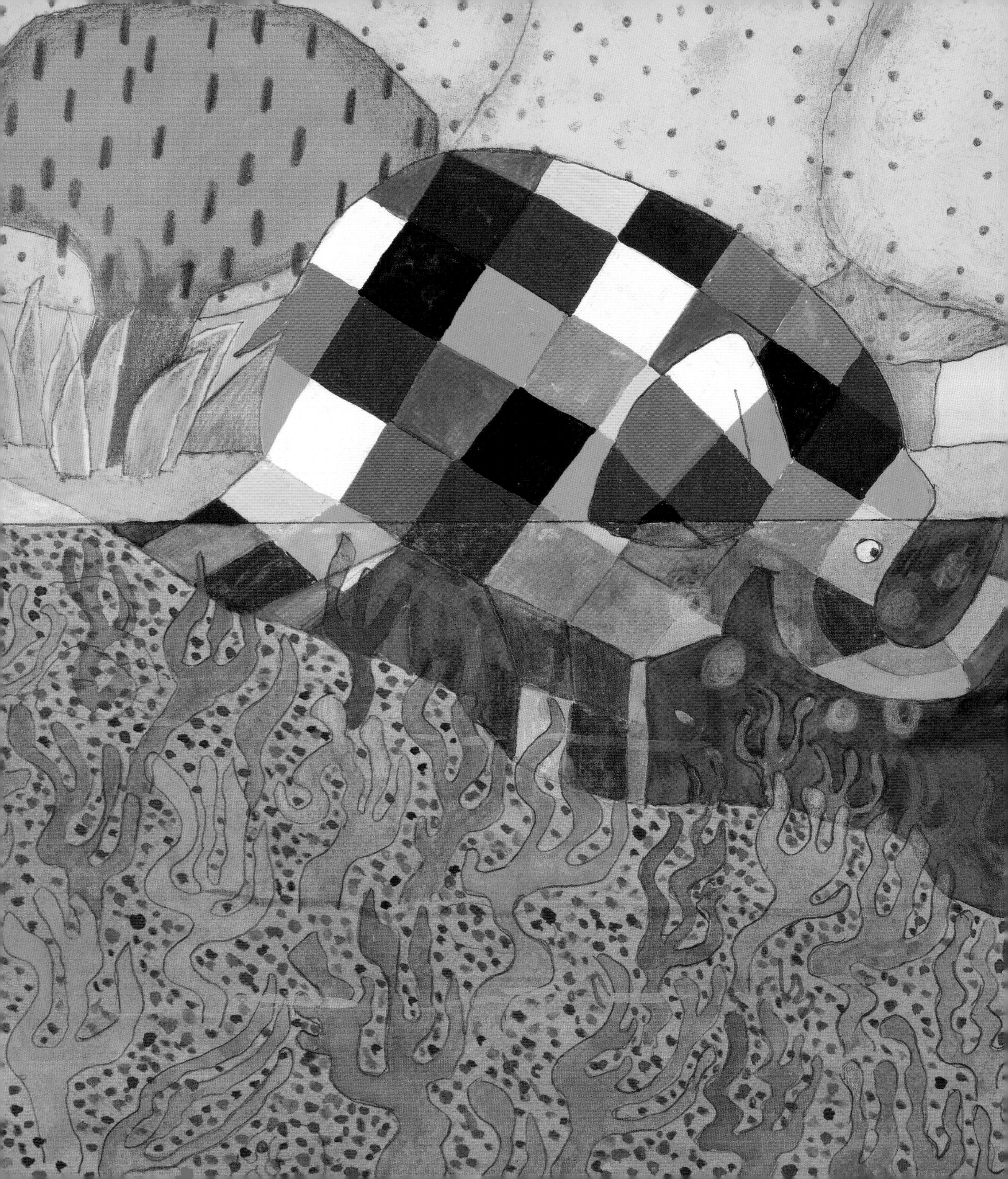

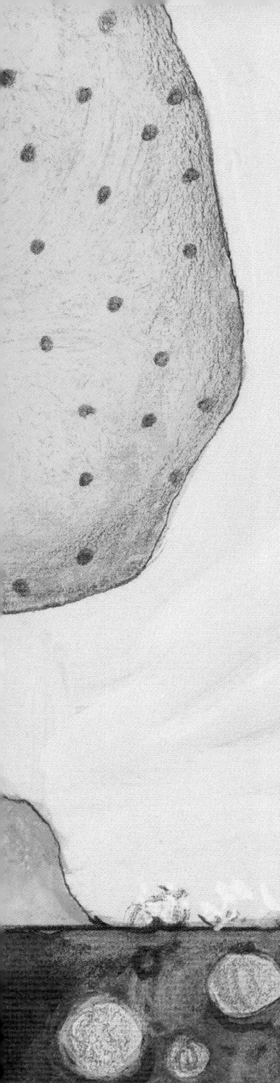

Farther along, Elmer thought he heard the tune coming from the lake.

"That's strange," he thought and put his head under the water. There was Crocodile bubbling Rose's tune. With a laugh, Elmer bubbled along with Crocodile for a moment before carrying on his walk.

Elmer was still humming when he heard Tiger.
"Hello Tiger," he said. "I think you've seen Rose."
"No," said Tiger in surprise. "Why do you say that?"
"The tune you're humming," said Elmer.
"Oh that," said Tiger. "When I passed Lion, he was humming it. Now I can't stop."

He'd just left Tiger when Elmer heard the tune coming from above him. The monkeys were humming together.

“Incredible,” thought Elmer. “We’re all humming Rose’s tune. I think I’ll have a quiet nap to get it out of my head.”

Elmer was awoken from his quiet
nap by the sound of loud talking.
The tune was still in his head as
he went to see what was going on.

“Hello Elmer,” said Lion. “We have a problem. It’s the tune—we can’t get it out of our heads.”
“Me either,” said Elmer. “I have an idea. Do any of you have a birthday today?” Nobody did. “Well, somebody somewhere does. Let’s sing ‘Happy Birthday’ together.”
“All right, Elmer,” said Tiger. “But you are funny.”

They started singing, timidly at first, but getting stronger and stronger as they went.

“Happy birthday to you, happy birthday to you. Happy birthday dear somebody, happy birthday to you.”

"Again and louder," said Elmer as Rose arrived and joined in. When they had finished the second time, he said, "And again."

They all sang it a third and fourth time, stopped, and burst out laughing.

"It worked," said Crocodile. "The tune has gone. Thanks, Elmer." Everyone echoed his words. "Thanks, Elmer." "Thanks, Elmer."

As the others went their various ways, Rose said, "I wonder whose birthday it was?"

A few days later, Lion and Tiger came by.
"Hello Elmer," said Lion. "We're trying to remember that tune. How did it go again?"
"I've forgotten," said Elmer.
"Pity," said Tiger. "It was a catchy little number."
And they left.

When they'd gone, the elephants roared with laughter.
"Well, I didn't want to start that again," said Elmer.

"But you'd think they'd know by now:
an elephant never forgets."

"You are naughty, Elmer," said an elephant. Then, still laughing, they chased him all the way home.